# Clementine's Treasure

### Annie White

Clementine was puzzled.
Something wasn't right.
The house was FAR too tidy,
her treasures out of sight.

There was vacuuming and dusting
and ironing as well
and through the house there floated
a most **delicious** smell.

There were sausage rolls and jam tarts,
a hundred cakes at least,

and **wibbly-wobbly** jelly –
a mouth-watering feast.

The amount of food, all in one room,
was more than she had seen!

But sadly it was not for her,
but someone called '**The Queen**'.

The Queen arrived at ten o'clock,
in time for morning tea.

She swept into the dining room,
a dream, all **glittery**.

'Hello!' she said to everyone,
'And who do we have here?
You must be Clementine,' she cooed.
'You really are a dear!'

Clementine had never seen
a more impressive sight.

That **sparkling** thing looked splendid
dancing in the light!

She headed for the garden
with her very **special** treasure.

The jewel was good to swing around,
she found to her great pleasure.

**Round** and **round** and **round** it sailed,

**sparkling** in the light,

and disappeared from sight.

when suddenly it **soared** right up

Meanwhile, the Queen was happily
sipping cups of tea,

when suddenly she noticed
she felt less **glitter-y**.

'The jewel the Corgis gave me,
the one I love so much!'
Everyone looked everywhere.
The Queen left in a **huff**.

The missing jewel was not indoors,
so next they searched outside.

'Clementine's found something!'
James and Granny cried.

The jewel was safely nestled
in a big, soft mound of **poo**.

Lots of soap and water

and it was good as **new**.

The Queen was overjoyed to see
her royal jewel once more.

And it seemed that now her jewel
was more **glittery** than before!

Baby's Room

Dining Room

Mum and Dad's Room

Lounge

Granny's Room

Bathroom

James' Room

Kitchen

For Lara and Daisy

First published in Great Britain in 2022 by Catch a Star,
an imprint of New Frontier Publishing Europe Ltd
Vicarage House, 58-60 Kensington Church Street, London W8 4DB
www.newfrontierpublishing.co.uk

Text and Illustrations copyright © 2022 Annie White
The moral rights of the author and illustrator have been asserted.

ISBN 978-1-913639-68-6

A CIP record for this book is available from the British Library

Edited by Tasha Evans • Designed by Verity Clark
Printed in Turkey

1 3 5 7 9 10 8 6 4 2